MR. TRIVIA
Presents

The Unofficial

STAR TREK
TRIVIA QUIZ

**Test Your Knowledge of the
Final Frontier—from Every Series and Film!**

A. L. ROGERS

3CG

ISBN 978-1-7362841-2-4

Published by 3CG/OHP, Sugarcreek, Ohio
cr3ativegroup@gmail.com

Star Trek

is the most expansive
science fiction universe. . .

. . .so your unofficial *Star Trek* trivia quiz should be, too! Test your knowledge of the greatest science fiction franchise ever with **Mr. Trivia Presents: The Unofficial Star Trek Trivia Quiz**.

These **300 questions**—thirty multiple-choice quizzes of ten questions each—will take you into deep space, where there are worlds filled with Klingons, Vulcans, Romulans, and Ferengi! Not to mention amazing technology. . .and endless possibilities.

What can you recall from *The Original Series* and *The Next Generation*? What do you remember from the newest shows, *Discovery*, *Picard*, and *Lower Decks*? And don't forget about the thirteen blockbuster movies!

Answers begin immediately after the thirtieth quiz—and each answer is accompanied by a snippet of bonus trivia. It's like your own personal starship computer (without the voice).

Enjoy your journey into the final frontier! **Live long and prosper!**

Quiz One
The Original Series: The Crew

1 Which member of the crew is known for his **fencing**?
  a) Chekov
  b) Sulu
  c) Scotty
  d) Spock

2 What are the names of **Mr. Spock's parents**?
  a) Ian and Lwaxana
  b) Jack and Beverly
  c) Trip and T'Pol
  d) Sarek and Amanda

3 What **US state** does Captain Kirk call home?
  a) California
  b) Kansas
  c) Ohio
  d) Iowa

4 Which member of the crew had his or her **memory erased** in "The Changeling"?
  a) Chekov
  b) Sulu
  c) Uhura
  d) Kirk

5 Which member of the crew was **secretly in love** with Mr. Spock?
  a) Nurse Chapel
  b) Yeoman Janice Rand
  c) Zarabeth
  d) Lt. Uhura

6 Which member of the crew is prone to make **dubious claims** about the achievements of his homeland?
    a) Scotty, of Scotland
    b) McCoy, of the South
    c) Spock, of the planet Vulcan
    d) Chekov, of Russia

7 What is the traditional **Vulcan salute**?
    a) palm out, fingers in a "V," separated between the middle and ring fingers
    b) palm out, fingers in a "V," separated between the middle and index fingers
    c) palm out, fingers together
    d) palm in, fingers in a "V," separated between the middle and ring fingers

8 Which one of these people was a **captain of the Enterprise** before Captain Kirk?
    a) Jean-Luc Picard
    b) John Harriman
    c) Christopher Pike
    d) Rachel Garrett

9 Why did Spock appear with a **goatee** in one episode?
    a) he was going undercover
    b) he was preparing for a Vulcan ritual
    c) he had been stranded for months at an abandoned starbase
    d) it was the mirror universe Spock, and he wore a goatee in his reality

10 Dr. McCoy once treated the wound of a **rock-like alien** with "thermal concrete." Which alien was it?
    a) the Gorn   c) the Horta
    b) Dilithium Bugs   d) Magnites

Quiz Two
The Original Series: Classic Episodes

1 In the episode "Operation—Annihilate!", what happened to **Kirk's brother**?

    a) he was arrested

    b) he died

    c) he was court martialed

    d) he returned from the future

2 Why must Spock **return to Vulcan** in "Amok Time"?

    a) for his wedding

    b) for his father's funeral

    c) for the birth of his child

    d) for his mother's funeral

3 What was the **first episode** called?

    a) "The Man Trap"

    b) "The Cage"

    c) "Encounter at Farpoint"

    d) "Shockwave"

4 Which **real-world topic** was explored by duo-chromatic aliens in "Let That Be Your Last Battlefield"?

    a) poverty   c) war

    b) racism   d) disease

5 What **kind of games** did the "Gamesters of Triskelion" like to play in an episode with the same name?

    a) gambling on gladiator games

    b) three-dimensional chess

    c) kadis-kot

    d) gambling at the dabo table

6 In "A Piece of the Action," Kirk, Spock, and McCoy visited a planet which had **adopted the culture** of which group from Earth history?

    a) Mayan warriors

    b) Civil War soldiers

    c) Chicago-style gangsters

    d) Wild West cowboys

7 **Which being** sent Kirk, Spock, and McCoy back in time in the acclaimed episode "The City on the Edge of Forever"?

    a) the Guardian of Forever

    b) the Caretaker

    c) the Custodian of Time

    d) the Guardian of the Edge

8 In "Tomorrow Is Yesterday" the *Enterprise* traveled back to 1969. **Who believed it was a UFO**?

    a) NASA   c) SpaceX

    b) the US Air Force   d) the National Guard

9 Which episode seemed to be **social commentary** on the Vietnam War?

    a) "Assignment: Earth"

    b) "Day of the Dove"

    c) "Let That Be Your Last Battlefield"

    d) "Private Little War"

10 **Which starship** was lost in "The Tholian Web," though a new model was featured years later in *Deep Space Nine*?

    a) USS *Rubicon*

    b) USS *Defiant*

    c) USS *Rio Grande*

    d) USS *Volga*

Quiz Three
The Original Series: Villains and Visitors

1 Which villain, introduced in "Space Seed," returned as the **antagonist of *Star Trek II*?**
    a) Harry Mudd
    b) Khan Noonien Singh
    c) Cyrano Jones
    d) mirror universe Sulu

2 Who was **Charlie** in "Charlie X" ?
    a) an android
    b) a baby
    c) an old man
    d) a teenager

3 What was the name of **Kirk's love interest** in "The City on the Edge of Forever" ?
    a) Dr. Gillian Taylor   c) Miramanee
    b) Janice Rand   d) Edith Keeler

4 In "Who Mourns for Adonais?" an alien claimed to be which figure from **Greek mythology**?
    a) Athena   c) Apollo
    b) Zeus   d) Artemis

5 Which famous **western characters** did the crew meet in "Spectre of the Gun?"
    a) Jesse James and Billy the Kid
    b) Jesse James and Butch Cassidy
    c) Wyatt Earp and Doc Holliday
    d) Wyatt Earp and Billy the Kid

6 "Balance of Terror" was a submarine-style battle between the *Enterprise* and a **warbird from which race**?

a) Romulans
b) Klingons
c) Cardassians
d) Tiburonians

7 In "Arena," Kirk battled a **lizard-like being** from which race?

a) Saurians
b) the Gorn
c) Velociraptors
d) the Draco

8 In "Wolf in the Fold," Scotty was accused of murdering a dancer, but it was an alien being who once also **possessed** whom?

a) "witches" in ancient Salem
b) the biblical figure, Cain
c) Jack the Ripper
d) Julius Caesar's assassin Brutus

9 In the first of his two appearances, what was **Harry Mudd** selling?

a) medical supplies
b) rare grain
c) weapons
d) women

10 While searching for a historian in "Patterns of Force," Captain Kirk and Spock were arrested by which earth **military force** of the past?

a) Roman soldiers
b) the US cavalry
c) Nazis
d) Knights of the Round Table

Quiz Four
The Original Series: Boldly Go

1 Which **registry numbers** were on the hull of the *Enterprise*?
   a) 1501
   b) 1601
   c) 1701
   d) 1801

2 **How long** was the USS *Enterprise*'s original mission?
   a) 5 years
   b) 10 years
   c) indefinite
   d) until they reached the farthest star in the galaxy

3 Nameless **security officers** were often killed or injured during away missions. What color shirts did they wear?
   a) red
   b) gold
   c) blue
   d) green

4 What did a **blue shirt** represent?
   a) science or engineering officer
   b) science or medical officer
   c) engineering or medical officer
   d) lieutenant or first officer

5 How often do Vulcans experience ***pon farr***, the irrepressible urge to mate?
   a) once in a lifetime
   b) once a year
   c) every seven years
   d) every seventy years

6 To whom did Spock give a **transfusion** in "Journey to Babel"?
- a) Surok
- b) Kirk
- c) McCoy
- d) Sarek

7 In how many episodes did **Diana Muldaur** appear?
- a) one
- b) two
- c) three
- d) four

8 What is described as a **"planet killer"** and nearly swallows the *Enterprise*?
- a) the Doomsday Machine
- b) the Infinity Gauntlet
- c) the Death Star
- d) the Armageddon Android

9 Which **important figure** from Federation history appeared for the first time in "Metamorphosis"?
- a) Surak
- b) T'Kuvma
- c) Dr. Soong
- d) Zefram Cochrane

10 Which member of the crew brought the **first tribble** on board the *Enterprise* in "The Trouble with Tribbles"?
- a) Uhura
- b) Chekov
- c) Lt. Kyle
- d) Rand

Quiz Five

The Next Generation: All about Picard

1 What did Captain Picard often say while **giving commands** to members of the crew?
- a) "Just do it."
- b) "There's no such thing as luck."
- c) "That's illogical."
- d) "Make it so."

2 What did Captain Picard often say when issuing an order to **move the *Enterprise***?
- a) "Engage"
- b) "Punch it!"
- c) "Let's go"
- d) "Vamoose!"

3 What kind of **beverage** did Captain Picard prefer?
- a) Tea. Earl Grey. Hot.
- b) Coffee, black
- c) Romulan ale
- d) Andorian mountain water

4 Which ship was under the **command of Captain Picard** before he was assigned to the *Enterprise*?
- a) USS *Bradbury*
- b) USS *Stargazer*
- c) USS *Titan*
- d) USS *Hathaway*

5 What does Captain Picard call **Commander Riker**?
- a) William
- b) Wesley
- c) F.O. (for First Officer)
- d) Number One

6 Which **instrument** did Captain Picard learn to play
in "The Inner Light"?
   a) guitar
   b) harp
   c) flute
   d) piano

7 Captain Picard served as the Arbiter of Succession during
the Klingon Civil War. Who did he appoint as the next
Chancellor?
   a) Lursa
   b) Kurn
   c) Gowron
   d) Worf

8 When Picard was **assimilated by the Borg**, what was
his new name?
   a) Locus   c) Lucias
   b) Lucas   d) Locutus

9 Under what circumstance did Picard shout, **"There are
four lights"**?
   a) when he was drugged by Romulans
   b) while he was tortured by a Cardassian
   c) when he was playing one of Q's "games"
   d) while saving the *Enterprise* from an unknown
      entity

10 Where was **Picard born**?
   a) Utopia Planetia (on Mars)
   b) Jupiter Station
   c) France
   d) England

Quiz Six
The Next Generation: The Crew, Part 1

1 How many members of the **bridge crew** (main characters) were not fully human?

      a) one   c) three

      b) two   d) four

2 Which two members of the crew wore red **uniforms** in season one, but gold uniforms in every other season?

      a) Worf and Wesley

      b) Worf and La Forge

      c) Riker and La Forge

      d) Data and Yar

3 Which member of the crew **was killed** during season one?

      a) Lieutenant Tasha Yar

      b) Reginald Barclay

      c) Ensign Robin Lefler

      d) Diana Giddings

4 Which member of the crew was not on board the *Enterprise* in season two, but **returned in season three** and stayed through the series finale?

      a) Worf

      b) Pulaski

      c) Dr. Crusher

      d) Riker

5 Deanna Troi's mother was a member of **which race** ?

      a) Betazoid

      b) Bajoran

      c) Trill

      d) Romulan

6 Which member of the crew could **see infrared and ultraviolet ranges**, among others?

    a) Lorca
    b) Troi
    c) Worf
    d) La Forge

7 Worf was the **"son of"** whom?

    a) Mogh
    b) Skywalker
    c) Sergey Rozhenko
    d) Kalis

8 What was the name of **Data's cat** ?

    a) Rex
    b) Spot
    c) Garfield
    d) Digit

9 Who was **Dr. Crusher's son** ?

    a) Paul
    b) Jack
    c) Wil
    d) Wesley

10 Who became the **chief engineer** after season one?

    a) La Forge
    b) Data
    c) O'Brien
    d) Worf

Quiz Seven
The Next Generation: The Crew, Part 2

1 Who **married** Miles O'Brien?
  - a) Tasha Yar
  - b) Keiko Ishikawa
  - c) Vash
  - d) Alyssa Ogawa

2 Who was the **bartender** onboard the *Enterprise*?
  - a) Quark
  - b) Wuher
  - c) Guinan
  - d) Malone

3 Which member of the crew was a **tap dancer and thespian**?
  - a) Picard
  - b) Dr. Crusher
  - c) Riker
  - d) Barclay

4 What **instrument** did Commander Riker play?
  - a) trombone
  - b) saxophone
  - c) clarinet
  - d) flute

5 What **species** was Ensign Ro Laren?
  - a) Orion
  - b) Betazoid
  - c) Bajoran
  - d) Trill

6 Which game were the **officers seen playing** during their off hours?
  - a) blackjack
  - b) Risk
  - c) dabo
  - d) poker

7 With whom did Riker have a **romantic relationship** before they were both assigned to the *Enterprise*?
  - a) Deanna Troi
  - b) Beverly Crusher
  - c) Ro Laren
  - d) Tasha Yar

8 Which **race** scattered Guinan's people?
  - a) Romulans
  - b) Klingons
  - c) Cardassians
  - d) the Borg

9 Who, more often than others, **sat at the helm** of the *Enterprise*?
  - a) Worf
  - b) La Forge
  - c) Data
  - d) Riker

10 What was Data's **main endeavor**?
  - a) to become more human
  - b) to serve in Starfleet
  - c) to be the first android captain
  - d) to find his creator

Quiz Eight
The Next Generation: Expanding Universe

1 What was the name of the **"pleasure planet"** ?
    a) Risa
    b) Betazed
    c) Viridian III
    d) Janus VI

2 Which **omnipotent character** was played by John de Lancie?
    a) the Squire of Gothos
    b) Q
    c) Thanos
    d) Doctor Manhattan

3 Which **actor from *Frasier*** played Captain Morgan Bateson in "Cause and Effect"?
    a) David Hyde Pierce
    b) Jane Leeves
    c) Kelsey Grammer
    d) John Mahoney

4 With whom did Vash have a **romantic relationship** ?
    a) Riker   c) Q
    b) Crusher   d) Picard

5 Which alien race said, **"Resistance is futile"** ?
    a) Cardassians
    b) the Borg
    c) Ferengi
    d) Romulans

6 Who was **Lore**?
  a) Worf's brother
  b) Data's brother
  c) a non-corporeal entity
  d) the name for Riker in the mirror universe

7 What did most **Borg vessels** look like?
  a) an arrowhead
  b) a blade
  c) a warbird
  d) a cube

8 What was the name of **Worf's son**?
  a) Kurn
  b) Alexander
  c) Napoleon
  d) Martok

9 Who **delivered** Miles O'Brien's baby?
  a) Worf
  b) Dr. Crusher
  c) Dr. Bashir
  d) Dr. Pulaski

10 Which **two races** used starships that look like birds?
  a) Klingons and Borg
  b) Romulans and Borg
  c) Romulans and Klingons
  d) Romulans and Vulcans

Quiz Nine

The Next Generation: Memorable Moments

1 What was the two-part **series finale** called?
    a) "Encounter at Farpoint"
    b) "All Good Things. . ."
    c) "To Boldly Go"
    d) "These Are the Voyages. . ."

2 Which **literary character** did Data play on the holodeck?
    a) Ebenezer Scrooge
    b) D'Artagnan
    c) Captain Ahab
    d) Sherlock Holmes

3 To which **literary setting** did Q transport the crew?
    a) Neverland
    b) Camelot
    c) Sherwood Forest
    d) Wonderland

4 Which supporting character suffered from **holo-addiction**—addiction to the holodeck and holograms?
    a) Reginald Barclay
    b) Wesley Crusher
    c) Miles O'Brien
    d) Alyssa Ogawa

5 When **the Traveler** appears, with which member of the crew does he spend most of his time?
    a) Deanna Troi
    b) Dr. Crusher
    c) Wesley Crusher
    d) Data

6 Which **member of the crew** from *The Original Series* did *not* appear in an episode of *The Next Generation*?
   - a) Kirk
   - b) Spock
   - c) McCoy
   - d) Scotty

7 **Finish this line** from the fan-favorite episode, "Darmok": "Darmok and Jalad. . ."
   - a) ". . .went to Risa."
   - b) ". . .at Tanagra."
   - c) ". . .stopped the Klingons."
   - d) ". . .went for milkshakes."

8 Who was the **antagonist** in both the series pilot and the series finale?
   - a) Gul Dukat
   - b) the Borg
   - c) Q
   - d) Gul Madred

9 Which ship **"stopped a war before it started"** by paying the ultimate price in "Yesterday's Enterprise"?
   - a) USS *Titan*
   - b) USS *Enterprise*-C
   - c) USS *Enterprise*-B
   - d) USS *Apollo*

10 Picard went undercover on Romulus **to find whom** in "Unification I and II"?
   - a) Riker
   - b) Vash
   - c) Data
   - d) Spock

Quiz Ten
Deep Space Nine: Cast and Crew

1 In which **famous battle** was Benjamin Sisko's wife killed?
   a) the Battle at the Wormhole
   b) the Deep Space Skirmish
   c) Battle at the Binary Stars
   d) Wolf 359

2 Which non-Klingon member of the crew was particularly **adept with a Klingon bat'leth**?
   a) O'Brien
   b) Sisko
   c) Dax
   d) Kira

3 Who were the **leaders of the Dominion**?
   a) the Founders
   b) the Clay
   c) Allmothers and Allfathers
   d) the Cardassians

4 What did the Bajorans call the **mysterious beings** that live in the wormhole?
   a) the Prophets
   b) the Creators
   c) the Provisional Government
   d) the Wormhole Aliens

5 Who became the **Grand Nagus of the Ferengi** in the final season?
   a) Quark
   b) Quark's brother, Rom
   c) Rom's son, Nog
   d) Glidia, the dabo girl

6 Which member of the crew from *The Next Generation* joined *Deep Space Nine* as **a series regular** in season four?

    a) Lt. Worf
    b) Chief O'Brien
    c) Ro Laren
    d) Commander Riker

7 Which member of the crew revealed that he or she was **genetically enhanced** as a child?

    a) Worf
    b) Odo
    c) Dax
    d) Bashir

8 In which **US city** did Benjamin Sisko's father own a restaurant?

    a) San Francisco
    b) Chicago
    c) New Orleans
    d) New York

9 With whom was Dr. Bashir **romantically involved** at the series' end?

    a) Jadzia Dax
    b) Kira Nerys
    c) Ezri Dax
    d) Nicole de Boer

10 What **kind of coffee** did Captain Sisko prefer to drink?

    a) black
    b) Racktajino
    c) Bajoran
    d) Vidiian blend, "a little bit of everything"

Quiz Eleven
Deep Space Nine:
Aliens on the Promenade

1 Who was **Leeta**?
- a) Quark's mother
- b) Quark's estranged daughter
- c) Quark's sister-in-law
- d) Quark's bookie

2 **What sport** did Captain Sisko love most?
- a) handball
- b) Bajoran football
- c) basketball
- d) baseball

3 Which species **occupied Bajor** and enslaved its people before the planet was liberated?
- a) the Maquis
- b) the Romulans
- c) the Ferengi
- d) the Cardassians

4 Who was frequently seen **sitting at Quark's bar** but never said a word?
- a) Morn
- b) Winn
- c) Kasidy
- d) Bareil

5 Which group of characters **traveled back in time** in "Little Green Men"?
- a) Kira, Odo, Quark and Rom
- b) Quark, Dukat, and Odo
- c) Quark, Rom, Nog and Odo
- d) Weyoun, Dukat, Sisko and Kira

6 Which Klingon, portrayed by J. G. Hertzler, became a **recurring character** in the final season?

    a) Martok
    b) Koloth
    c) Kor
    d) Kang

7 Who eventually led the **Cardassian Liberation Front** against the Dominion?

    a) Gul Dukat
    b) Damar
    c) Gul Madred
    d) Tora Ziyal

8 Which recurring character was portrayed by **Marc Alaimo**?

    a) Morn
    b) Gul Dukat
    c) Vedek Bareil
    d) Rom

9 Which of these Starfleet officers **attacked the *Defiant*** as a member of the Maquis?

    a) Kasidy Yates
    b) Ro Laren
    c) Michael Eddington
    d) Chakotay

10 **What species** was Weyoun?

    a) Broca
    b) Lorca
    c) Horta
    d) Vorta

Quiz Twelve
Deep Space Nine:
Adventures at the Wormhole

1 What were the **small cruisers** called that the crew frequently used for travel in their area of the galaxy?
- a) shuttlepods
- b) runabouts
- c) salamanders
- d) transports

2 What was the name of the **small, agile battleship** that is assigned to *Deep Space Nine*?
- a) the *Defiant*
- b) the *Ganges*
- c) the *Rio Grande*
- d) the *Yukon*

3 Which race was **addicted** to Ketracel-white?
- a) Ferengi
- b) Romulans
- c) Andorians
- d) Jem'Hadar

4 What was ***Deep Space Nine*** called before the Federation took command of the station?
- a) Station K-7
- b) the Gate of Bajor
- c) Terok Nor
- d) Mos Eisley Spaceport

5 In which episode was the crew **stuck inside** a James Bond holosuite program?
- a) "Our Man Bashir"
- b) "Hippocratic Oath"
- c) "Body Parts"
- d) "Bar Association"

6 Which character was suspected to be **a spy**—or perhaps a former spy?
- a) Morn
- b) Dr. Bashir
- c) Kira Nerys
- d) Elim Garak

7 In the two-part episode "Homefront" and "Paradise Lost," who **secretly infiltrated** the Federation on Earth?
- a) Cardassians
- b) the Jem'Hadar
- c) the Founders
- d) the Maquis

8 Which member of the crew was led to believe he or she had **been in prison** for twenty years?
- a) Kira
- b) O'Brien
- c) Odo
- d) Bashir

9 Who was the **first Ferengi** in Starfleet?
- a) Quark
- b) Rom
- c) Nog
- d) Gint

10 What was the **primary conflict** of the final story arc of the series?
- a) the Klingon Civil War
- b) the Dominion War
- c) the Invasion of Bajor
- d) the Destruction of the Wormhole

Quiz Thirteen
Voyager: A Motley Crew

1 Which **group of rebels** did Chakotay, B'Elanna Torres, and
many other members of the crew belong to before joining
the crew of *Voyager*?

     a) the Bajoran Resistance
     b) the Amerinds
     c) the Maquis
     d) the Rebellion

2 In the series pilot, why was Tom Paris **in custody**?

     a) arson—he destroyed the Crystalline Entity
     b) treason—he joined the Maquis
     c) perjury—he lied under oath about a failed
        mission
     d) grand theft spacecraft—he stole a starship

3 What was **Seven of Nine**'s real name?

     a) Alice Krige   c) Jeri Ryan
     b) Annika Hansen   d) Erin Hansen

4 **Which member** of *Voyager*'s crew was also a member
of Captain Sulu's crew on the *Excelsior*?

     a) Tuvok   c) Neelix
     b) the Doctor   d) Janeway

5 What was the name of the **girl born on *Voyager*,**
who then became a recurring character?

     a) Brooke Stephens
     b) Vanessa Branch
     c) Scarlett Pomers
     d) Naomi Wildman

6 **What species** was Neelix?
    a) Ocampan   c) Talaxian
    b) Kazon   d) Malon

7 Which **US state** did Captain Kathryn Janeway call home?
    a) Indiana   c) Missouri
    b) Iowa   d) Ohio

8 What was the name of the **alien being** that pulled *Voyager* across the galaxy in the series pilot?
    a) the Watcher
    b) the Caretaker
    c) the Guardian of Forever
    d) the Creator

9 In the series pilot, why did Captain Janeway **destroy the array**, the powerful machine that could have sent *Voyager* home?
    a) to stop a Borg invasion
    b) to prevent the Jem'Hadar from entering the Alpha Quadrant
    c) to prevent the Kazon from gaining control of it
    d) "Oops. That button must be the photon torpedoes. . ."

10 Which member of *Voyager*'s crew was **never promoted** beyond the rank of ensign—even after seven seasons?
    a) the Doctor
    b) Paris
    c) Crusher
    d) Kim

Quiz Fourteen
Voyager: Species of the Delta Quadrant

1 Which members of *Voyager*'s crew **eventually married**?
    a) Kes and Neelix
    b) Chakotay and Janeway
    c) Seven and Tuvok
    d) Paris and Torres

2 **Which race** was divided into multiple, warring sects?
    a) the Kazon
    b) the Vidiians
    c) the Ocampa
    d) the Nacene

3 In season six, Seven of Nine took care of a **group of children** across multiple episodes. Why?
    a) to learn to be a mother
    b) because they were holograms
    c) because they were her children from the future
    d) because they were also ex-Borg

4 Which member of *Voyager*'s crew **left the ship** (and the regular cast) at the beginning of season four?
    a) Chakotay   c) Seven of Nine
    b) Kes   d) Barclay

5 What was the name of the **small spacecraft** specially designed on *Voyager*?
    a) the *Ganges*
    b) the *Galileo Seven*
    c) *Shuttlepod One*
    d) the *Delta Flyer*

6 What did **the Doctor say** whenever his program was activated?

a) "Rule 1: the Doctor lies."
b) "Please state the nature of the medical emergency."
c) "If this is a medical emergency, please call 9-1-1."
d) "I'm a doctor, not a psychiatrist!"

7 Which member of *Voyager*'s crew had a father who was **a Starfleet admiral**?

a) Janeway
b) Kim
c) Paris
d) Torres

8 **Which version** of the Emergency Medical Hologram was the Doctor?

a) Mark 1
b) Mark 2
c) Mark 3
d) Mark 4

9 Which **recurring character** from *The Next Generation* worked to contact *Voyager* from Starfleet headquarters in San Francisco?

a) Deanna Troi
b) Reginald Barclay
c) Miles O'Brien
d) Keiko O'Brien

10 Which instrument did **Harry Kim play**-?

a) violin
b) guitar
c) clarinet
d) saxophone

Quiz Fifteen

Voyager: "To the Journey!"

1 **What did *Voyager* have** that the *Enterprise*-D did not?
   a) food replicators
   b) warp nacelles
   c) bio-neural circuitry
   d) a chair for the first officer next to the
      captain's chair

2 **The Hirogen** were known in the Delta Quadrant as what?
   a) traders
   b) hunters
   c) weapons manufacturers
   d) cloners

3 Who had **transwarp** conduits?
   a) Vulcans   c) the Borg
   b) Caretakers   d) Kazon

4 Which **dimension of space** did Species 8472 inhabit?
   a) fluidic space
   b) inside black holes
   c) the Badlands
   d) mirror universe

5 What was the name of Tom Paris's **holodeck character**
   who battled nefarious villains in a black-and-white,
   B-movie setting?
   a) Captain Neutron
   b) Captain Dilithium
   c) Captain Marvel
   d) Captain Proton

6 What was the name of the young, male, **ex-Borg drone** who became a recurring character in season seven?
   a) Mezoti
   b) Icheb
   c) Azan
   d) Rebi

7 Seska was a secret operative, genetically altered to appear human. **What species** was she?
   a) Klingon
   b) Romulan
   c) Cardassian
   d) Andorian

8 What did Captain Janeway **prefer to drink**?
   a) Romulan ale
   b) coffee
   c) tea
   d) orange juice

9 Which member of the crew trained to become the Doctor's **medical assistant**?
   a) Kes
   b) Seven of Nine
   c) Paris
   d) Samantha Wildman

10 In the series finale "Endgame," the **Doctor of the future** had finally picked a name for himself. What was it?
   a) Jack
   b) Jim
   c) John
   d) Joe

Quiz Sixteen
Enterprise : Warp Capable

1 Which **species** was Dr. Phlox?
- a) Talaxian
- b) Denobulan
- c) Kelpien
- d) Klingon

2 What were the **hull numbers** on Captain Archer's *Enterprise*?
- a) NX-01
- b) NX-1701
- c) ENT-01
- d) NX-01-A

3 Who was the **tactical officer**?
- a) Travis Mayweather
- b) Major Hayes
- c) Charles Tucker III
- d) Malcolm Reed

4 At the end of the mirror universe episodes, who emerged as the **leader of the Terran Empire**?
- a) Empress Sato
- b) Emperor Archer
- c) Emperor Reed
- d) Empress T'Pol

5 Which species was **secretly studying humanity** before they made first contact?
- a) Betazoids
- b) Cardassians
- c) Vulcans
- d) El-Aurians

6 What was **Captain Archer's father**?
- a) inventor of the tricorder
- b) designer of the transporter
- c) developer of the warp five engine
- d) creator of the first holodeck

7 Who was **Porthos**?
- a) the ship's onboard computer
- b) Captain Archer's beagle
- c) Dr. Phlox (his first name)
- d) the fourth Musketeer

8 **Which character** did Brent Spiner play in *Enterprise*?
- a) Dr. Arik Soong
- b) Dr. Noonian Soong
- c) Lore
- d) Data

9 Which **six-species alien race** was determined to destroy Earth in the third season?
- a) the Gormogon
- b) the Borg
- c) Species 8472
- d) the Xindi

10 What did Dr. Phlox like to **use during treatments**, which often made the crew suspicious?
- a) unusual chemical combinations
- b) alien plants
- c) live animals
- d) powerful Denobulan drugs

Quiz Seventeen
Enterprise : Faith of the Heart

1 What did **Commander Tucker**'s friends call him?
- a) Chief
- b) Tuck
- c) Trip
- d) Chuck

2 With whom did T'Pol have a **romantic relationship**?
- a) Reed
- b) an Orion
- c) Archer
- d) Tucker

3 Which member of the crew was **born in space**?
- a) Sato
- b) Tucker
- c) Reed
- d) Mayweather

4 Which species was **never shown** in an episode of this series?
- a) Romulan
- b) Klingon
- c) Tellarite
- d) Orion

5 What was the **maximum speed** of Archer's *Enterprise*?
- a) Warp speed
- b) Warp 2
- c) Warp 5
- d) Warp 9

6 Crewman Daniels was not who he appeared to be—across several episodes he helped Archer **fight in what**?
- a) the Xindi Conflict
- b) the Temporal Cold War
- c) the Klingon War for Gagh
- d) the Epic Dabo Extravaganza

7 Which **supporting cast member** from *Deep Space Nine* portrayed the Andorian Shran?
- a) J. G. Hertzler
- b) Andrew Robinson
- c) Jeffrey Combs
- d) Wallace Shawn

8 Which **onboard member of the crew** was never named beyond his or her role?
- a) "Chef"
- b) "Chief"
- c) "Constable"
- d) "Nurse"

9 In the fourth season, Captain Archer carried the *katra* of which **famous Vulcan**?
- a) Spock
- b) Surak
- c) Sarek
- d) Soval

10 Which **characters from *The Next Generation*** appeared in the series finale?
- a) La Forge and Data
- b) Data and Guinan
- c) Picard and Troi
- d) Riker and Troi

Quiz Eighteen
Discovery : *Discovery*'s Crew

1 Who is the **captain of the *Discovery*** in season one?
  a) Gabriel Lorca
  b) Christopher Pike
  c) Philippa Georgiou
  d) Michael Burnham

2 Which species is **Mr. Saru**?
  a) Tellarite
  b) Tholian
  c) Xindi
  d) Kelpien

3 Which member of the crew was **found on an asteroid** in the crashed USS *Hiawatha* in season two?
  a) Ash Tyler   c) Lt. Detmer
  b) Jett Reno   d) Linus

4 Who **raised Michael Burnham** after her biological parents were killed?
  a) Spock's parents
  b) Kirk's parents
  c) Uhura's parents
  d) Noonian Soong

5 What **moniker** did Michael Burnham earn before being reinstated?
  a) Starfleet's first traitor
  b) Starfleet's first murderer
  c) Starfleet's first insurrectionist
  d) Starfleet's first mutineer

6 To **which planet** must the crew take Adira Tal in season three?
- a) Vulcan
- b) Earth
- c) Trill
- d) Ni'Var

7 Who **sits at the helm**, even after suffering an injury that forced him or her to wear ocular implants?
- a) Tilly
- b) Detmer
- c) Owo
- d) Bryce

8 Which member of the crew was killed and later **resurrected**?
- a) Culber
- b) Detmer
- c) Bryce
- d) Tilly

9 Which character is a **Klingon/human hybrid**?
- a) Tyler
- b) Airiam
- c) Lorca
- d) Linus

10 Which member of the crew is **"the Slayer of Sorna Prime"** in the mirror universe?
- a) Burnham
- b) Lorca
- c) Tilly
- d) Giorgeou

Quiz Nineteen
Discovery : The Future Is Now

1 What is the **name of the battle** that takes place in episode one of season one?
- a) Wolf 359
- b) the Battle of the *Shenzhou*
- c) the Battle of the Binary Stars
- d) the Battle for Sector 001

2 **What device** enables the *Discovery* to travel in a way unlike any other Starfleet vessel?
- a) the Hyper Drive
- b) the Spore Drive
- c) the Warp Drive
- d) the Hard Drive

3 What **kind of alert** does the *Discovery* go to before traveling through the mycelial network?
- a) Black alert
- b) Red alert
- c) Yellow alert
- d) Blue alert

4 What is the **mysterious being** the crew chases throughout season two?
- a) the Red Angel
- b) Tartigrade
- c) the Klingon chancellor
- d) the Crystalline Entity

5 Mirror universe Georgiou joins **which group** in season two?
- a) the Xindi
- b) Romulan Star Empire
- c) Section 31
- d) Obsidian Order

6 Who **broke out of a psychiatric unit** on Starbase 5 in season two?

a) Saru   c) Kirk

b) Burnham   d) Spock

7 **How many years** did the crew travel into the future in season three?

a) 700 years   c) 1,000 years

b) 930 years   d) 3,188 years

8 How long was Michael **searching for the *Discovery*** in the future before she found it?

a) one month   c) three years

b) one year   d) five years

9 What was **"the burn"** ?

a) the day Section 31 attacked Starfleet headquarters

b) the day the androids destroyed Mars, decimating its population

c) the day starships across the galaxy were suddenly destroyed as their dilithium went inert and destroyed their warp cores

d) the day the Klingon moon, Praxis, was destroyed

10 Ni'Var is the homeworld to **which species** in season three?

a) Vulcans and Romulans

b) Vulcans and Klingons

c) Romulans and Klingons

d) Vulcans and Romulans and Klingons

Quiz Twenty
Picard : The Legend Returns

1 Which **cyberneticist** was killed in "Stardust City Rag"?
  a) Flint
  b) Agnes Jurati
  c) Bruce Maddox
  d) Dr. Daystrom

2 Seven of Nine was forced to kill **an ex-Borg drone** she called "my child." Who was that?
  a) Naomi Wildman
  b) Icheb
  c) an unnamed character
  d) Eight of Nine

3 What was the name of **Captain Rios's ship** ?
  a) *ibn Majid*
  b) *Baxial*
  c) *Defiant*
  d) *La Sirena*

4 Why did Raffi **visit Stardust City** in "Stardust City Rag"?
  a) to reconcile with her son
  b) to reconcile with her mother
  c) to reconcile with her sister
  d) to reconcile her taxes

5 Which **member of the crew** of the *Enterprise*-D was acting captain of the *Zheng He* in "Et in Arcadia, Part 2"?
  a) La Forge
  b) Worf
  c) Data
  d) Riker

6   What was the **relationship** between Narek and Narissa?
   a) siblings
   b) lovers
   c) friends
   d) clones

7   Which **guest star** from *The Next Generation* episode
   "I, Borg" returned in this series?
   a) Dr. Crusher
   b) Guinan
   c) Hugh
   d) the Borg Queen

8   What were **former Borg drones** called?
   a) Ex-B's
   b) Ex-Drones
   c) New Individuals
   d) Ex-D's

9   **Which sport** did Captain Rios love to play?
   a) handball
   b) soccer
   c) springball
   d) Parisses Squares

10   Who was Dr. **Altan Inigo Soong**?
   a) Noonian Soong's human son
   b) Noonian Soong's brother
   c) Noonian Soong's twin
   d) Noonian Soong's final android

Quiz Twenty-One

The Original Series Films:
New Life

1 What was the name of **Spock's half-brother** in *The Final Frontier*?

    a) Saavik   c) Sarek

    b) Sybok   d) T'Pring

2 To which **prison colony** were Captain Kirk and Dr. McCoy sent to in *The Undiscovered Country*?

    a) Alcatraz

    b) the Dilithium mines of Remus

    c) the Dilithium mines of Rura Penthe

    d) the spice mines of Kessel

3 Which did Captain Kirk **sell to a pawn shop** in order to get 20th century money in *The Voyage Home*?

    a) tricorder

    b) communicator

    c) phaser

    d) reading glasses

4 What were the names of **the whales** in *The Voyage Home*?

    a) Gene and Majel

    b) George and Gracie

    c) Will and Deanna

    d) Willie and Shamu

5 **Which song** was played at Spock's funeral service in *The Wrath of Khan*?

    a) "The Sounds of Silence"

    b) the *Star Trek* theme song

    c) "Amazing Grace"

    d) a Vulcan burial dirge

6 Who was **famous for saying**, "the needs of the many outweigh the needs of the few"?
- a) Spock
- b) Sarek
- c) Kirk
- d) Scotty

7 In **which vessel** did Kirk and company travel back in time in *The Voyage Home*?
- a) a Klingon Bird-of-Prey
- b) the Guardian of Forever
- c) the *Enterprise*
- d) a DeLorean

8 What was the name of the **terraforming device** in *The Wrath of Khan*?
- a) the Harvester
- b) Terra One
- c) the Positronic Brain
- d) Genesis

9 Who was **"conscripted"** to rejoin the crew of the *Enterprise* by Captain Kirk in *The Motion Picture*?
- a) Bones
- b) Spock
- c) Scotty
- d) Chekov

10 What was **"the undiscovered country"** the sixth film, *The Undiscovered Country*, was referring to?
- a) the Neutral Zone
- b) the future
- c) subspace
- d) the Delta Quadrant

Quiz Twenty-Two
The Original Series Films:
New Civilizations

1 In which film did Kirk, Scotty, and the others **steal the *Enterprise*?**

    a) *Star Trek: The Motion Picture*
    b) *Star Trek II: The Wrath of Khan*
    c) *Star Trek III: The Search for Spock*
    d) *Star Trek IV: The Voyage Home*

2 What was the name of **Hikaru Sulu's ship** in *The Undiscovered Country*?

    a) USS *Excelsior*
    b) USS *Titan*
    c) USS *Shenzhou*
    d) USS *Enterprise*

3 **What role** had Mr. Spock assumed for the Federation in *The Undiscovered Country*?

    a) vice admiral   c) commodore
    b) special envoy   d) ambassador

4 In addition to McCoy, who was **also a doctor** on the *Enterprise* in *The Motion Picture*?

    a) Pavel Chekov   c) Phil Boyce
    b) M'Benga   d) Christine Chapel

5 Who was **Captain Kirk's son**?

    a) Samuel Kirk
    b) David Marcus
    c) Samuel Marcus
    d) Marcus Kirk

6 What was McCoy carrying **inside his mind** in *The Search for Spock*?

    a) Spock's repressed emotions
    b) the secret of Project Genesis
    c) Spock's *katra*
    d) an alien nanite

7 In *The Final Frontier,* the *Enterprise* crosses the Great Barrier. Who was **supposed to reside** beyond this barrier?

    a) the Chancellor of the Klingon Empire
    b) the lifeform V'Ger
    c) the Vulcan teacher Surak
    d) God

8 Who was the **new captain** of the *Enterprise* in *The Motion Picture*?

    a) Will Decker
    b) John Harriman
    c) Rachel Garrett
    d) Hikaru Sulu

9 Who portrayed the Klingon antagonist, **Commander Kruge**, in *The Search for Spock*?

    a) Brock Peters
    b) David Warner
    c) Christopher Plummer
    d) Christopher Lloyd

10 What historic **peace treaty** was signed in *The Undiscovered Country*?

    a) the Interstellar Law
    b) the Neutral Zone Treaty
    c) the Khitomer Accords
    d) the Treaty of Organia

Quiz Twenty-Three
The Next Generation Films: The Crew Returns

1 What did Geordi install **inside Data** in *Generations*?
    a) a new positronic relay
    b) a trilithium scanner
    c) the complete *Enterprise* computer files
    d) an emotion chip

2 Who **directed** *Insurrection*?
    a) Brannon Braga
    b) Brent Spiner
    c) Jonathan Frakes
    d) David Twohy

3 **Which song** did Data sing at Riker and Troi's wedding in *Nemesis*?
    a) "Here Comes the Bride"
    b) "Blue Skies"
    c) "Fly Me to the Moon"
    d) "The Nearness of You"

4 Who **sat at the helm** of the *Enterprise*-B in *Generations*?
    a) Kirk's son
    b) Chekov's son
    c) Spock's half-brother
    d) Sulu's daughter

5 Who was promoted to **lieutenant commander** on the holodeck, on a seafaring ship?
    a) Wesley
    b) Worf
    c) Data
    d) O'Brien

6 Which **character from *Voyager*** appeared in *First Contact*?
   a) the Doctor
   b) Seven of Nine
   c) Admiral Janeway
   d) Neelix

7 In which film did **Worf say**, "I have an odd craving for the blood of a live *kolar* beast"?
   a) *Generations*
   b) *First Contact*
   c) *Insurrection*
   d) *Nemesis*

8 What did Geordi **see for the first time** with his own eyes in *Insurrection*?
   a) the stars
   b) the warp car
   c) a sunrise
   d) the faces of his best friends

9 Who got **comically drunk** in *First Contact*?
   a) the Borg
   b) Riker
   c) Data
   d) Troi

10 What did Riker do to his **trademark beard** in *Insurrection*?
   a) shave it off
   b) tailor it to a goatee
   c) let it run wild and free, like a bunnicorn at a dabo table
   d) encourage it to join Starfleet and save the Federation from beardless captains

Quiz Twenty-Four
The Next Generation Films:
Big Screen Problems

1 From which **section of the *Enterprise*** did the Borg seize control in *First Contact*?
  a) main engineering
  b) the bridge
  c) the transporter rooms
  d) Ten Forward

2 What was the name of the **energy ribbon** in *Generations*?
  a) the Tholian Web
  b) Unimatrix Zero
  c) the Wave
  d) the Nexus

3 Which member of the crew was **ignoring Starfleet protocol** in the beginning of *Insurrection*?
  a) Riker   c) La Forge
  b) Data   d) Worf

4 **What deck** was Kirk on when the *Enterprise*-B was hit?
  a) the bridge
  b) the cargo bay
  c) deck fifteen
  d) deck eight

5 What was the unique **area of space** called in *Insurrection*?
  a) the Briar Patch
  b) the Badlands
  c) Negative Space
  d) the Bermuda Triangle

6 **Which song** did Captain Picard sing with Data while flying shuttles?

    a) "The Major-General's Song"
    b) "Do-Re-Mi"
    c) "A British Tar"
    d) "When I Was a Lad"

7 In which film was the **saucer section separated** from the rest of the ship?

    a) *Generations*
    b) *First Contact*
    c) *Insurrection*
    d) *Nemesis*

8 What was the name of **the android** found in *Nemesis*?

    a) B-4
    b) Lore
    c) Meta Data
    d) Lal

9 Which two **people groups** were at war in *Insurrection*?

    a) the Klingons and the Romulans
    b) the Cardassians and the Bajorans
    c) the Tellarites and the Andorians
    d) the Son'a and the Ba'ku

10 What was the name of **Zefram Cochrane's ship** in *First Contact*?

    a) *Titan II*
    b) *Enterprise*
    c) *Phoenix*
    d) *Apollo*

Quiz Twenty-Five
The Next Generation Films: Villains and Guest Stars

1 **Which villain** appeared for the first time in *First Contact*, then appeared in later episodes of *Voyager*?

   a) Seska
   b) Species 8472
   c) the Borg Queen
   d) Annorax

2 How did Admiral Matthew Dougherty **meet his ghastly demise** in *Insurrection*?

   a) He was thrown out of an airlock.
   b) His skin was stretched until he died.
   c) His beating heart was removed from his body.
   d) He was forced to ingest dilithium.

3 Which **award-winning actor** portrayed Dr. Soran in *Generations*?

   a) Ian McKellan
   b) Tom Hardy
   c) Christopher Lloyd
   d) Malcolm McDowell

4 Who was **Shinzon of Remus**?

   a) Captain Picard's clone
   b) Captain Picard's estranged son
   c) the Romulan villain who also appeared in
      Star Trek (2009)
   d) the mirror universe Picard

5 Which actress **from Disney's *Tangled*** portrayed Anij in *Insurrection*?

   a) Mandy Moore
   b) Donna Murphy
   c) Delaney Rose Stein
   d) Kristen Bell

6 Which **pair of Klingons** met their end in *Generations*?
    a) Kor and Koloth
    b) Antaak and Krell
    c) Lursa and B'Etor
    d) Martok and Kang

7 Which **actor from *Parks and Rec*** appeared as a member of the USS *Defiant* crew in *First Contact*?
    a) Adam Scott
    b) Chris Pratt
    c) Nick Offerman
    d) Aziz Ansari

8 Who, besides Captain Kirk, **appeared to Captain Picard** in the Nexus?
    a) Troi
    b) Vash
    c) Q
    d) Guinan

9 Which **Academy Award-nominated actor** appeared as Zefram Cochrane in *First Contact*?
    a) Glenn Corbett
    b) James Cromwell
    c) Alfre Woodard
    d) Tom Hardy

10 Which member of the crew made the **ultimate sacrifice** in *Nemesis*?
    a) Riker
    b) Troi
    c) La Forge
    d) Data

Quiz Twenty-Six
Kelvin Timeline Films:
An Alternate Reality

1   What event **created the new timeline** for these films?
>   a) A Romulan ship from the future was destroyed by the USS *Kelvin,* beginning a war between the Federation and the Romulan Star Empire.
>   b) A Romulan ship traveled back in time and destroyed the USS *Kelvin.*
>   c) Prime reality Spock traveled back in time to save a planet from destruction, creating a "schism in time" and allowing the new reality to exist.
>   d) Crewman Daniels traveled back in time and commandeered the USS *Kelvin* to end the Temporal Cold War, destroying the *Kelvin* and inadvertently creating a new timeline.

2   Which of Kirk's **love interests** appeared in *Into Darkness* ?
>   a) Antonia   c) Carol Marcus
>   b) Miramanee   d) Edith Keeler

3   What **BBC star** portrayed antagonist Khan in *Into Darkness* ?
>   a) Benedict Cumberbatch   c) Mark Gatiss
>   b) Martin Freeman   d) Andrew Scott

4   Which of the following **planets was destroyed** in the *Kelvin* timeline films?
>   a) Mars   c) Vulcan
>   b) Kronos   d) Tellar Prime

5   With which member of the crew did Mr. Spock have a **romantic relationship**?
>   a) Lt. Uhura   c) Dr. Culber
>   b) Ensign Syl   d) Nurse Chapel

6 *Into Darkness* opened with the crew **saving a pre-warp culture** from death. How?
  a) diverting an asteroid from making impact
  b) freezing an erupting volcano
  c) sharing a cure for a deadly virus
  d) preventing an invasion

7 **Which actor** from *The Original Series* cast was seen in all three *Kelvin* timeline films?
  a) William Shatner
  b) Nichelle Nichols
  c) Walter Koenig
  d) Leonard Nimoy

8 What was the name of the **crashed federation starship** in *Beyond*?
  a) USS *Defiant*
  b) USS *Franklin*
  c) USS *Antares*
  d) ISS *Enterprise*

9 Which **father figure** in Captain Kirk's life was killed in *Into Darkness*?
  a) Samuel Kirk
  b) Robert April
  c) Christopher Pike
  d) Admiral Marcus

10 What was the name of Scotty's **alien companion**?
  a) Venser
  b) Wee Laddie
  c) Keenser
  d) Dewey

Quiz Twenty-Seven
Kelvin Timeline Films:
A Bright Future

1 What was the name of the **Starfleet test** Kirk rigged in *Star Trek*?
- a) the Kobayashi Maru Scenario
- b) the Starfleet entrance exam
- c) the Neutral Zone Scenario
- d) the No-Win Scenario

2 Bones observed that **Vulcans have their hearts** where humans have their what?
- a) kidneys
- b) stomach
- c) spleen
- d) liver

3 Which alien did **Bones revive** with Khan's "superblood" in *Into Darkness*?
- a) a Gorn
- b) a tribble
- c) a Horta
- d) a salt vampire

4 How did Jaylah **describe her music** to Scotty in *Beyond*?
- a) alien sounds
- b) as "classical" music
- c) beats and shouting
- d) loud and distracting

5 Who **gave his life** to fix the warp core in *Into Darkness*?
- a) Spock
- b) Kirk
- c) Khan
- d) Scotty

6 Who was the **primary antagonist** in *Beyond*?
    a) Krall
    b) Nero
    c) Khan
    d) Manas

7 What was the name of the **new starbase** in *Beyond*?
    a) Starbase 243
    b) New London
    c) Deep Space 12
    d) Yorktown

8 Which actor of **Marvel movie fame** portrayed George Kirk in *Star Trek*?
    a) Chris Hemsworth
    b) Chris Evans
    c) Jeremy Renner
    d) Clark Gregg

9 Which member of the cast **co-wrote *Beyond***?
    a) Zachary Quinto
    b) John Cho
    c) Simon Pegg
    d) Karl Urban

10 In the *Kelvin* timeline, Scotty **developed a formula** for what?
    a) trilithium fusion
    b) transwarp beaming
    c) "hyperspeed"
    d) the spore drive

Quiz Twenty-Eight
The Animated Series: *Star Trek*'s Kahs-wan

1 **Cyrano Jones** returned in which episode?
  a) "The Survivor"
  b) "Mudd's Passion"
  c) "More Tribbles, More Trouble"
  d) "The Pirates of Orion"

2 The alien Arex replaced **which member** of the original crew?
  a) Sulu   c) Uhura
  b) Chekov   d) Bones

3 What was a *sehlat*?
  a) an alien visitor
  b) a member of the crew
  c) a Starfleet rank
  d) a Vulcan pet

4 **Which being** sent Spock back to his childhood in "Yesteryear"?
  a) the Guardian of Forever
  b) Q
  c) Surak
  d) the Squire of Gothos

5 What was the name of the **female, cat-like alien** member of the crew?
  a) Karla Five
  b) Majel
  c) T'Pol
  d) M'Ress

6 In "Bem," Captain Kirk's **middle name** was revealed to be what?
   a) Thomas
   b) Titanus
   c) Tiberillus
   d) Tiberius

7 When the men of the *Enterprise* fell to the all-female aliens in "The Lorelei Signal," **who took charge**?
   a) Rand
   b) Chapel
   c) Uhura
   d) M'Ress

8 Which **Klingon character** returned in "The Time Trap"?
   a) Kor
   b) General Chang
   c) Koloth
   d) Worf

9 How many **episodes** were in the second and final season?
   a) four
   b) six
   c) ten
   d) twelve

10 In the final episode the **"first captain of the Enterprise"** is onboard. What was his name?
   a) Christopher Pike
   b) Jonathan Archer
   c) Robert April
   d) James Doohan

Quiz Twenty-Nine
Short Treks: A New Frontier

1 Which **actor from *The Office*** directed "The Escape Artist"?
 a) Rainn Wilson
 b) John Krasinski
 c) Mindy Kaling
 d) B. J. Novak

2 Which **highly reproductive creature** was injected with human DNA in the "The Trouble with Edward"?

a) rabbit	c) tribble
b) tardigrade	d) *sehlat*

3 When Ensign Spock and Number One were stuck in a turbo lift in "Q&A," **which song** did they sing?
 a) "Blue Skies"
 b) "I Am the Very Model of a Modern Major General"
 c) "Oh, On the Starship *Enterprise*"
 d) "It's the End of the World"

4 What **brought the two girls together** in "Children of Mars"?
 a) an attack on Mars
 b) a fight at their school
 c) distance from their parents
 d) pet tribbles

5 Which **member of the crew** from *Star Trek: Discovery* appeared in "The Girl Who Made the Stars"?
 a) Lt. Commander Airiam
 b) Joann Owosekun
 c) Michael Burnham
 d) Keyla Detmer

6 Who was **the prisoner** in "Ask Not"?
a) Dr. Soran
b) Khan Noonien Singh
c) Kruge
d) Christopher Pike

7 Which **major event** from an *Original Series* film occurred at the end of "Ephraim and Dot"?
a) the *Enterprise* self-destructs
b) the death of Spock
c) the death of Captain Kirk
d) Qo'noS explodes

8 In "The Brightest Star," **who made first contact** with Mr. Saru?
a) Michael Burnham
b) Philippa Georgiou
c) Gabriel Lorca
d) Spock

9 What did **the stowaway Po create** in "Runaway" that made relations with her planet become suddenly valuable to others in the galaxy?
a) spore drive
b) dilithium incubator
c) transwarp drive
d) a holodeck

10 **How long** had the USS *Discovery* been holding position in "Calypso"?
a) 1 year
b) 50 years
c) 500 years
d) 1,000 years

Quiz Thirty

Lower Decks: Where No Comedy Has Gone Before

1 What was the **name of the ship** ?
- a) USS *Enterprise*
- b) USS *Roddenberry*
- c) USS *Saratoga*
- d) USS *Cerritos*

2 What was **Beckett Mariner's secret** in season one?
- a) The captain is her sister.
- b) The captain is her father.
- c) The captain is her mother.
- d) The captain is her aunt.

3 Which member of the crew was **an Orion** ?
- a) D'Vana Tendi
- b) Brad Boimler
- c) Beckett Mariner
- d) Samanthan Rutherford

4 **Which race** was the security officer?
- a) Human
- b) Bajoran
- c) Klingon
- d) Vulcan

5 In the opening credits, the ship was shown **fleeing a battle** with whom?
- a) Andorians
- b) the Borg
- c) Klingons
- d) Q

6 Which **actress from *Space Force*** voiced Beckett Mariner?
  a) Lisa Kudrow
  b) Diana Silvers
  c) Tawny Newsome
  d) Punam Patel

7 Which **famous antagonist** made a cameo appearance in "Veritas," saying, "Can you prove that humanity is worth saving?"
  a) Apollo
  b) a Founder
  c) Khan
  d) Q

8 **What is unique** about Samanthan Rutherford?
  a) He has cybernetic implants.
  b) He is a Borg drone.
  c) He is an Ex-B.
  d) He is another creation of Dr. Soong.

9 What does the chief medical officer, **Commander T'Ana**, look like?
  a) a humanoid insect
  b) a humanoid canine
  c) a humanoid feline
  d) a humanoid lizard

10 **Which members** of *The Next Generation* crew appeared in the season one finale?
  a) Data and La Forge
  b) Riker and Troi
  c) Picard and Riker
  d) Picard and Worf

Quiz One Answers
The Original Series: The Crew

1. **B** (Mr. Sulu. See "The Naked Time" from season one.)

2. **D** (Sarek and Amanda. One a Vulcan and one a human.)

3. **D** (Kirk was from Iowa, though William Shatner is Canadian.)

4. **C** (Lt. Uhura. The object responsible was called *Nomad.*)

5. **A** (Nurse Chapel. See "The Naked Time" among others.)

6. **D** (Throughout the series Chekov claimed that Russians could be credited for many great achievements, even when others corrected him.)

7. **A** (Leonard Nimoy said he based the salute on a Jewish gesture.)

8. **C** (Christopher Pike. See "The Menagerie" and "The Menagerie, Part II" from season one.)

9. **D** (The episode "Mirror, Mirror" was the first appearance of the mirror universe, where so much is different from *Star Trek*'s prime reality, including Spock's style.)

10. **C** (This fan-favorite episode was titled "The Devil in the Dark.")

Quiz Two Answers

The Original Series: Classic Episodes

1. **B** (George Samuel "Sam" Kirk died in "Operation—Annihilate!")

2. **A** (He was betrothed to a Vulcan named T'Pring.)

3. **A** ("The Man Trap," which included Captain Kirk. The original pilot, "The Cage," wasn't aired until years later. Among many differences, Kirk was not the captain.)

4. **B** (Characters Lokai and Bele had skin that was white on one side of the face and black on the other.)

5. **A** (The games were played by captives whom they referred to as "thralls.")

6. **C** (The "gangster" culture was based on a book called *Chicago Mobs of the Twenties.*)

7. **A** (When Kirk asked, "Are you machine or being?" the Guardian of Forever said "I am both and neither.")

8. **B** (According to the captain's log, the "high gravitational attraction" of a nearby "black star" sent the *Enterprise* to 1969.)

9. **D** (In "Private Little War" Klingons gave advanced weaponry to a pre-warp planet.)

10. **B** (The *Defiant* featured in *The Original Series* was a *Constitution*-class starship. The *Defiant* in *Deep Space Nine* was the prototype of a new class.)

Quiz Three Answers
The Original Series: Villains and Visitors

1. **B** (Khan. Actor Ricardo Montalban portrayed him in both appearances.)

2. **D** (This teenager had superhuman powers granted to him by Thasians.)

3. **D** (Keeler was portrayed by Joan Collins, who later starred in *Dynasty.*)

4. **C** ("Apollo" grabbed the *Enterprise* in space with a giant green hand!)

5. **C** (The crew experienced a "spectre" of the shootout at the O.K. Corral.)

6. **A** ("Balance of Terror" was the first appearance of Romulans in the *Star Trek* franchise.)

7. **B** (An alien race called the Metrons forced Kirk into a one-on-one battle with a Gorn captain.)

8. **C** (This lifeform had many names, including Redjac.)

9. **D** (The episode was titled "Mudd's Women.")

10. **C** (The Nazi society was thriving on a planet called Ekos, where Ekosians oppressed Zeons.)

Quiz Four Answers
The Original Series: Boldly Go

1. **C** (The full registry for the *Enterprise* in *The Original Series* was NCC-1701.)

2. **A** (5 years. Listen closely to Captain Kirk's monologue during the theme song.)

3. **A** (Scotty and Uhura wore red uniforms too, though neither were security officers.)

4. **B** (Spock and Bones wore blue; science and medical respectively.)

5. **C** (Spock said *pon farr* is "a thing no outworlder may know" and that it "transcends even the discipline of the service [to Starfleet].")

6. **D** (Sarek was Spock's estranged father.)

7. **B** (Muldaur played two different characters in *The Original Series*, and a third character in *The Next Generation*.)

8. **A** ("The Doomsday Machine" was the name of the planet killer and the episode, which included commentary on the real-world Cold War.)

9. **D** (Cochrane's importance to the Federation was developed in other shows and films, most notably *The Next Generation* film, *First Contact*.)

10. **A** (Uhura was given the first tribble by Cyrano Jones.)

Quiz Five Answers
The Next Generation: All about Picard

1. **D** (Only the internet knows how many times he said, "Make it so." Many, many times.)

2. **A** ("Engage" was also the name of the official *Star Trek* podcast.)

3. **A** (Earl Grey gets its distinct flavor from bergamot oil, a citrus fruit from the Mediterranean region.)

4. **B** (See "The Battle" from season one.)

5. **D** (He also calls his dog "Number One" in *Picard.*)

6. **C** (This fan-favorite episode provides viewers a sense of what Picard might have been like as a family man.)

7. **C** (Gowron is one of a handful of characters portrayed by Robert O'Reilly.)

8. **D** (His full name was Locutus of Borg. See "The Best of Both Worlds," parts I and II.)

9. **B** (This occurred in the lauded episode "Chain of Command, Part II")

10. **C** (France is correct, in spite of his British accent.)

Quiz Six Answers
The Next Generation: The Crew, Part 1

1. **C** (Worf, Troi, and Data.)

2. **B** (Worf and La Forge both changed roles and responsibilities while on the *Enterprise*-D, leading to changes in their uniforms.)

3. **A** (Yar was killed by the being Armus in "Skin of Evil.")

4. **C** (Viewers are told that Dr. Crusher was the head of Starfleet Medical during that time.)

5. **A** (Troi's father was human.)

6. **D** (Via his VISOR, or Visual Instrument and Sensory Organ Replacement.)

7. **A** (Rozhenko was the surname for his adoptive human father, but Worf was called "Worf, son of Mogh," which is a reference to his biological Klingon father.)

8. **B** (Spot is in many episodes and even survives a deadly crash in *Generations.*)

9. **D** (Wesley is fifteen years old in season one.)

10. **A** (Before La Forge was promoted, he was a conn officer.)

Quiz Seven Answers
The Next Generation: The Crew, Part 2

1. **B** (Keiko was portrayed by Rosalind Chao in *The Next Generation* and *Deep Space Nine.*)

2. **C** (The bar was in a crew lounge called Ten Forward.)

3. **B** (Dr. Crusher taught Data to tap dance in "Data's Day.")

4. **A** (See especially "11001001" from season one.)

5. **C** (Laren's personal history involved the occupation of Bajor, which was described in numerous episodes of *Deep Space Nine.*)

6. **D** (Even junior officers played poker in season seven's "Lower Decks.")

7. **A** (Did these star-crossed lovers ever get together? See *Nemesis.*)

8. **D** (See "I Borg" especially, from season five.)

9. **C** (Data typically sat to Picard's left.)

10. **A** (This was a running theme in the series, but "The Measure of a Man" is a key episode.)

Quiz Eight Answers
The Next Generation:
Expanding Universe

1. **A** (Risa appeared or was referenced in numerous episodes. "Captain's Holiday" from season three is among the most memorable.)

2. **B** (Q was a member of the Q Continuum, a race of godlike beings.)

3. **C** (Patrick Stewart likewise appeared in an episode of *Frasier,* "The Doctor Is Out.")

4. **D** (Vash's romance with Captain Picard began on Risa.)

5. **B** (The Borg first appeared in "Q Who?" from season two.)

6. **B** (Lore was portrayed by Brent Spiner.)

7. **D** (In *Picard,* an abandoned Borg cube is called simply, "the Artifact.")

8. **B** (Alexander's mother, K'Ehleyr, was half human and half Klingon.)

9. **A** (Worf delivered Molly in Ten Forward.)

10. **C** (The ships were called Romulan warbirds and Klingon Birds-of-Prey.)

Quiz Nine Answers
The Next Generation: Memorable Moments

1. **B** (Both parts were first aired on May 21, 1994.)

2. **D** (On other occasions, Data also played the king in Shakespeare's *Henry V* and Prospero from *The Tempest*.)

3. **C** (See "Qpid" from season four.)

4. **A** (See "Hollow Pursuits" and "The Nth Degree." This addiction became a defining part of Barclay's story.)

5. **C** (Wesley resigned from Starfleet to be mentored by the Traveler.)

6. **A** (Kirk and Picard did not cross paths until the film *Generations*.)

7. **B** (The line refers to two strangers who defeated a common enemy.)

8. **C** (In the series finale Q said the trial against humanity, which took place in the series pilot, had never actually ended.)

9. **B** (Picard famously said in this episode, "Let's make sure history never forgets the name *Enterprise*.")

10. **D** (Spock was secretly attempting to reunite the Vulcans and Romulans.)

Quiz Ten Answers

Deep Space Nine: Cast and Crew

1. **D** (This was the devastating battle initiated by Locutus of Borg.)

2. **C** (Worf preferred the mek'leth.)

3. **A** (The Founders were changelings, as was Constable Odo.)

4. **A** (Many of the non-Bajoran characters called them "wormhole aliens.")

5. **B** (Rom was portrayed by Max Rodénchik.)

6. **A** (See "The Way of the Warrior" parts I and II in season four.)

7. **D** (The practice was illegal when Bashir's parents decided to do it.)

8. **C** (The restaurant was called Sisko's Creole Kitchen or just Sisko's.)

9. **C** (Ezri Dax was portrayed by Nicole de Boer.)

10. **B** (Raktajino is Klingon coffee. Drink it with honor!)

Quiz Eleven Answers
Deep Space Nine:
Aliens on the Promenade

1. **C** (Leeta was portrayed by Chase Masterson.)

2. **D** (A baseball was visible on Sisko's desk in most episodes and he talked about watching classic games in the holosuites.)

3. **D** (The first mention of the Cardassian occupation of Bajor occurred in "Ensign Ro," part of season five of *The Next Generation.*)

4. **A** (His name is an anagram of Norm, a barfly character from *Cheers.*)

5. **C** (They mistakenly traveled to Roswell, New Mexico, in 1947.)

6. **A** (The characters in the other three answers appeared together in "Blood Oath.")

7. **B** (He was portrayed by Casey Biggs.)

8. **B** (Alaimo also portrayed the first Cardassian ever shown in the *Star Trek* franchise, Gul Macet.)

9. **C** (See "For the Uniform" in season five.)

10. **D** (Most of the Weyoun were portrayed by Jeffrey Combs.)

Quiz Twelve Answers
Deep Space Nine:
Adventures at the Wormhole

1. **B** (Runabouts were typically considered to be bigger than shuttlecraft, which were aboard starships like the *Enterprise.*)

2. **A** (The ship first appeared on *Deep Space Nine* in season three, "The Search, Part I.")

3. **D** (Their addiction was genetically engineered.)

4. **C** (It was a Cardassian design and a remnant of the occupation of Bajor.)

5. **A** (The 1966 film "Our Man Flint" is another parody of the James Bond franchise.)

6. **D** (Garak was indeed once a member of the Obsidian Order, a Cardassian intelligence agency.)

7. **C** (The Founders had infiltrated the Federation, though the human Admiral Leyton caused significant problems in those episodes.)

8. **B** (In "Hard Time" from season four.)

9. **C** (Sisko endorsed Nog's application to Starfleet Academy.)

10. **B** (The conflict caused great destruction to Cardassia Prime and prompted the Treaty of Bajor.)

Quiz Thirteen Answers
Voyager: A Motley Crew

1. **C** (The Maquis. Answer B, Amerind, is a planet in *The Original Series,* "The Paradise Syndrome.")

2. **B** (Paris was in New Zealand at a Federation penal settlement.)

3. **B** (Seven of Nine's real name was Annika Hansen. Seven/Hansen was portrayed by Jeri Ryan.)

4. **A** (Tuvok was the science officer. See the episode, "Flashback.")

5. **D** (The other answers are actors who portrayed Naomi Wildman; most often it was Scarlett Pomers.)

6. **C** (Neelix grew up on the planet Talax's moon, Rinax.)

7. **A** (Janeway was born in Bloomington, Indiana.)

8. **B** (In the series pilot the Caretaker appeared to the crew as a banjo playing human.)

9. **C** (The pilot first aired on January 16, 1995.)

10. **D** (Ensigns Ro and Crusher were each on board the *Enterprise*-D at different times.)

Quiz Fourteen Answers
Voyager: Species of the Delta Quadrant

1. **D** (In the final season, Torres was expecting their child.)

2. **A** (There were eighteen different Kazon sects, fighting over natural resources.)

3. **D** (The children first appeared in "Collective.")

4. **B** (Kes propelled *Voyager* out of Borg space when she left.)

5. **D** (Paris led the design of this craft.)

6. **B** (Answer A belongs to another famous sci-fi doctor.)

7. **C** (Owen Paris, who was most often portrayed by Richard Herd.)

8. **A** (See, especially, "Life Line" in season six.)

9. **B** (Barclay was portrayed by Dwight Schultz, who also had a regular role on *The A-Team*.)

10. **C** (Data, from the *Enterprise*-D, could play the violin.)

Quiz Fifteen Answers
Voyager: "To the Journey!"

1. **C** (The ship's bio-neural gel packs were infected with a virus in "Learning Curve.")

2. **B** (See them hunt Species 8472 in "Prey.")

3. **C** (These conduits were featured in the series finale, "Endgame.")

4. **A** (There are no stars in fluidic space. Only organic matter.)

5. **D** (Harry Kim played his sidekick, Buster Kincaid.)

6. **B** (Mezoti, Azan and Rebi are other ex-Borg children who appeared in fewer episodes.)

7. **C** (Seska was portrayed by Martha Hackett.)

8. **B** (Janeway prefers to drink her coffee black.)

9. **A** (Kes was portrayed by Jennifer Lien.)

10. **D** (Paris ribbed him for picking such a common name after all those years.)

Quiz Sixteen Answers
Enterprise: Warp Capable

1. **B** (From the planet Denobula, a polyamorous culture.)

2. **A** (The registry numbers in answer D, NX-01-A, are for the USS *Dauntless*. See the *Voyager* episode "Hope and Fear.")

3. **D** (Portrayed by Dominic Keating.)

4. **A** (The episodes appeared in season four; "In a Mirror, Darkly," parts I and II.)

5. **C** (See "Carbon Creek" from season two.)

6. **C** (His name was Henry Archer and he worked closely with Zefrem Cochrane.)

7. **B** (Porthos was a dog that loved to eat cheese.)

8. **A** (Dr. Arik Soong was an ancestor of Dr. Noonian Soong, who would create Data.)

9. **D** (Xindi-Aquatics, Xindi-Arboreals, Xindi-Insectoids, Xindi-Primates, Xindi-Reptilians, and the Xindi-Avians, who were extinct.)

10. **C** (Phlox once cauterized a wound by sticking an osmotic eel on his patient. See "Minefield" from season two.)

Quiz Seventeen Answers
Enterprise: Faith of the Heart

1. **C** ("Trip" as in "triple" because he was Charles Tucker III.)

2. **D** (Romance bloomed during Vulcan neuro-pressure sessions.)

3. **D** (Mayweather was born and raised on a cargo freighter.)

4. **A** (The first time humans saw a Romulan happened years later in the *Star Trek* timeline, in *The Original Series*, "Balance of Terror.")

5. **C** (For comparison, Picard's *Enterprise* could achieve warp 9, and sometimes more.)

6. **B** (Crewman Daniels was from the 31st century.)

7. **C** (Combs portrayed numerous characters on *Deep Space Nine,* but none were Andorian.)

8. **A** (His face is only shown in the series finale, but it wasn't his actual face. It was the face of someone posing as his character in a holodeck simulation.)

9. **B** (In *The Original Series* episode "The Savage Curtain," Spock called Surak "the greatest of all who ever lived on our planet.")

10. **D** (The series finale was titled "These Are the Voyages. . .")

Quiz Eighteen Answers
Discovery : *Discovery*'s Crew

1. **A** (He was played by Jason Isaacs.)

2. **D** (Saru was the first Kelpien to join Starfleet.)

3. **B** (Reno was portrayed by Tig Notaro.)

4. **A** (Burnham is Spock's foster sister.)

5. **D** (See "Context Is for Kings" for the use of this moniker.)

6. **C** (See season three's "Forget Me Not.")

7. **B** (Keyla Detmer piloted both the *Shenzhou* and the *Discovery*.)

8. **A** (From the episode "Saints of Imperfection.")

9. **A** (The Klingon, Voq, underwent a procedure to make himself appear as the human Ash Tyler, which included keeping his DNA, memories, and consciousness.)

10. **C** (Ensign Tilly's mirror universe counterpart was an infamous and deadly starship captain.)

Quiz Nineteen Answers
Discovery : The Future Is Now

1. **C** (Burnham started this battle with a life-altering decision.
See the series pilot.)

2. **B** (Paul Stamets theorized and helped create the spore drive.)

3. **A** (The ship is only at black alert for a few seconds when it
makes a "jump" through the mycelial network from one location
to another.)

4. **A** (The Red Angel was a human time traveler.)

5. **C** (Georgiou from the prime universe was killed, so there was no
chance for her to cross paths with her counterpart.)

6. **D** (Spock was portrayed by Ethan Peck, grandson of famed actor
Gregory Peck.)

7. **B** (See "That Hope Is You, Part 1.")

8. **B** (Burnham spent most of this year traveling with Book and
Grudge.)

9. **C** (This catastrophic event nearly destroyed the Federation.)

10. **A** (Ni'Var is the new name for the planet Vulcan. See
"Unification III.")

Quiz Twenty Answers
Picard : The Legend Returns

1. **C** (Maddox was portrayed by John Ales, a new actor for the character.)

2. **B** (Icheb first appeared in the *Voyager* episode "Collective" and became a recurring character.)

3. **D** (In English *La Sirena* is translated as "siren" or sometimes "mermaid.")

4. **A** (Raffi's surname was Musiker.)

5. **D** (Riker boasted that it was "the toughest, fastest, most powerful ship Starfleet ever put into service.")

6. **A** (These siblings were also Romulan spies.)

7. **C** (Hugh was portrayed in both series by Jonathan Del Arco.)

8. **A** (Ex-B's were "butchered" for their parts by the criminal Bjayzl.)

9. **B** (Rios loved soccer, but various characters on *Deep Space Nine* played springball.)

10. **A** (This Soong was of course portrayed by Brent Spiner.)

Quiz Twenty-One Answers
The Original Series Films:
New Life

1. **B** (Sybok was portrayed by actor Laurence Luckinbill.)

2. **C** (Rura Penthe, not Remus, which was a planet in the Romulan system.)

3. **D** (Kirk's reading glasses were a gift from Bones early in the film.)

4. **B** (A combination of real whales and models were used to create George and Gracie.)

5. **C** (Scotty performed "Amazing Grace" on the bagpipes during Spock's funeral.)

6. **A** (Mr. Spock. These were some his last words before his death.)

7. **A** (The Bird-of-Prey was commandeered in the previous film, *The Search for Spock.*)

8. **D** (Genesis; a word that means "origin" or the "coming into being" of something.)

9. **A** (Bones was "conscripted." Scotty and Chekov were still active in Starfleet. Spock rejoined the crew later, of his own volition.)

10. **B** (A phrase in Shakespeare's *Hamlet* describes the future as "the undiscovered country.")

Quiz Twenty-Two Answers
The Original Series Films:
New Civilizations

1. **C** (They steal the *Enterprise* from spacedock, risking their future standing as Starfleet officers.)

2. **A** (The *Excelsior* is also featured in the *Voyager* episode, "Flashback.")

3. **B** (As special envoy, Spock was handling diplomatic communications with the Klingon Empire.)

4. **D** (Dr. Chapel and Dr. McCoy both monitor Spock in sickbay after his attempted mind meld with V'Ger.)

5. **B** (David Marcus was portrayed by Merritt Butrick, who also appeared in *The Next Generation* episode "Shades of Gray.")

6. **C** (Spock's *katra* was reunited with his body during a Vulcan ritual in *The Search for Spock.*)

7. **D** (The entity was not God, though at first Sybok was convinced it was.)

8. **A** (Will Decker was quickly relieved of his post by Admiral Kirk.)

9. **D** (Lloyd is perhaps best known for his role in the *Back to the Future* films, the first of which released in 1985, one year after *The Search for Spock.*)

10. **C** (The Khitomer Accords are referenced throughout the *Star Trek* franchise. Peace between the Klingon Empire and the Federation leads to many things, including Worf joining Starfleet.)

Quiz Twenty-Three Answers
The Next Generation Films:
The Crew Returns

1. **D** (The emotion chip first appeared in *The Next Generation* episode "Brothers.")

2. **C** ("Number One" also directed *First Contact.*)

3. **B** (B-4 reprised the song at the end of the film.)

4. **D** (Her name was Demora Sulu.)

5. **B** (Worf was promoted from lieutenant to lieutenant commander.)

6. **A** (It was not technically the same Doctor, but another hologram from the Emergency Medical Holographic program.)

7. **C** (Thankfully, no *kolar* beasts were injured during the making of *Insurrection.*)

8. **C** (Geordi was standing on the Ba'ku homeworld when he saw it.)

9. **D** (Troi was drinking tequila with Zefram Cochrane.)

10. **A** (When Data noticed Riker's cleanshaven face, Riker said, "Smooth as an android's bottom.")

Quiz Twenty-Four Answers
The Next Generation Films: Big Screen Problems

1. **A** (*First Contact* was the first film to feature the *Enterprise*-E.)

2. **D** (One character described the Nexus in this way: "It was like being inside joy.")

3. **B** (Data exposed a secret research facility containing Starfleet personnel.)

4. **C** (Kirk told Captain Harriman to stay on the bridge.)

5. **A** ("Briar Patch" was a name given to this region of space by Dr. Arik Soong in *Enterprise* episode "The Augments.")

6. **C** (It was from the comic opera *H.M.S. Pinafore.*)

7. **A** (The saucer section also separated from the ship in *The Next Generation* series pilot, "Encounter at Farpoint.")

8. **A** (B-4 and Lore were both Data's "brothers.")

9. **D** (The Son'a were once Ba'ku but were in exile.)

10. **C** (The *Phoenix* was the first human ship to achieve warp.)

Quiz Twenty-Five Answers
The Next Generation Films:
Villains and Guest Stars

1. **C** (Alice Krige portrayed the character in *First Contact* and *Voyager*'s "Endgame.")

2. **B** (Dougherty was portrayed by Anthony Zerbe of *Omega Man* fame.)

3. **D** (Dr. Soran is an El-Aurian, as is Guinan.)

4. **A** (Shinzon was portrayed by Tom Hardy, who also played the villains Bane and Venom in DC and Marvel films.)

5. **B** (Murphy has won two Tony Awards for best actress in a musical.)

6. **C** (Riker issued the order to fire which destroyed their ship.)

7. **A** (Scott is an unnamed helm officer.)

8. **D** (Picard met an "echo" of his favorite bartender in the Nexus.)

9. **B** (Cromwell was nominated for Best Supporting Actor in the film *Babe*.)

10. **D** (Data was aboard the Romulan ship *Scimitar* when it was destroyed.)

Quiz Twenty-Six Answers
Kelvin Timeline Films:
An Alternate Reality

1. **B** (Kirk's father was killed when the *Kelvin* was destroyed, further altering the timeline.)

2. **C** (The prime reality version of Dr. Marcus appeared in *The Wrath of Khan* and *The Search for Spock.*)

3. **A** (Cumberbatch portrayed the title character in the BBC's *Sherlock.*)

4. **C** (Spock's mother, Amanda Grayson, died in the *Kelvin* timeline during the destruction of Vulcan.)

5. **A** (Uhura was portrayed by Zoe Saldana.)

6. **B** (Spock set off a cold fusion device while standing inside the erupting volcano.)

7. **D** (Nimoy appeared as prime reality's Spock in *Star Trek* and *Into Darkness.* The actor's image was shown, as Spock, in *Beyond.*)

8. **B** (The USS *Franklin* was the first Earth ship capable of reaching warp 4.)

9. **C** (Pike talked Kirk into joining Starfleet in the first film.)

10. **C** (Keenser was portrayed by veteran actor Deep Roy, who also portrayed Yoda for second unit shots in *The Empire Strikes Back* and *Return of the Jedi.*)

Quiz Twenty-Seven Answers
Kelvin Timeline Films:
A Bright Future

1. **A** ("Kobayashi Maru " is not only the name of the scenario, but also the name of a ship within the simulation.)

2. **D** (Bones says this in *Beyond*.)

3. **B** (Khan was genetically enhanced, giving his blood regenerative capabilities.)

4. **C** (The song used to disrupt the enemy ships was "Sabotage" by the Beastie Boys.)

5. **B** (The scene was an inverse of a similar scene in *The Wrath of Khan*.)

6. **A** (Krall was once a Starfleet captain named Balthazar Edison.)

7. **D** (Bones called it a "snow globe in space, waiting to break.")

8. **A** (Hemsworth portrayed Thor in numerous Marvel Studios films.)

9. **C** (Pegg, who portrayed Scotty, is a huge fan of *The Original Series*.)

10. **B** (In the first film Scotty described transwarp beaming as "like trying to hit a bullet with a smaller bullet, whilst wearing a blindfold, riding a horse.")

Quiz Twenty-Eight Answers
The Animated Series: *Star Trek*'s Kahs-wan

1. **C** (Jones first appeared in *The Original Series* episode, "The Trouble with Tribbles.")

2. **B** (Walter Koenig is not part of the cast, but he wrote the episode "The Infinite Vulcan.")

3. **D** (As a child, Spock had a *sehlat* named I-Chaya. It is shown in *The Animated Series* but first referenced in *The Original Series* episode, "Journey to Babel.")

4. **A** (The Guardian of Forever was first seen in *The Original Series* episode, "The City on the Edge of Forever.")

5. **D** (The character was voiced by Majel Barrett.)

6. **D** (This was the first time his middle name was revealed. *The Original Series* only referenced his middle initial: James T. Kirk.)

7. **C** (Answer A, Yeoman Rand, is the only character in this list that did not appear in *The Animated Series*.)

8. **A** (Kor also appears in *Deep Space Nine*'s "Blood Oath.")

9. **B** (The final episode premiered on October 12, 1974.)

10. **C** (April's wife, Sarah, was the ship's chief medical officer.)

Quiz Twenty-Nine Answers
Short Treks: A New Frontier

1. **A** (Wilson was also the star of the episode.)

2. **C** (It was Lt. Edward Larkin's DNA.)

3. **B** (The song is from Gilbert and Sullivan's *The Pirates of Penzance.*)

4. **A** (The attack on Mars was part of the storyline in season one of *Picard.*)

5. **C** (Kenric Green was the voice of her father, Mike Burnham.)

6. **D** (Pike was portrayed by Anson Mount.)

7. **A** (Other events from *The Original Series* were shown, including a scene from "Space Seed.")

8. **B** (Viewers were also introduced to Mr. Saru's sister, Siranna.)

9. **B** (Her home planet was Xahea.)

10. **D** (The ship had been empty all that time and the episode does not explain why.)

Quiz Thirty Answers
Lower Decks: Where No Comedy Has Gone Before

1. **D** (Cerritos is a city in [real world] southern California.)

2. **C** (The captain's name was Carol Freeman.)

3. **A** (Tendi was voiced by Noël Wells.)

4. **B** (His name was Lieutenant Shaxs.)

5. **B** (Borg cubes were battling Romulan warbirds as the *Cerritos* flees.)

6. **C** (Newsome portrayed Captain Angela Ali in *Space Force.*)

7. **D** (Q was voiced by the inimitable John de Lancie.)

8. **A** (Rutherford's implants were installed by Vulcans.)

9. **C** (T'Ana is Caitian, the same "cat people" species as M'Ress from *The Animated Series.*)

10. **B** (Riker and Troi appeared onboard the USS *Titan.*)

About the Author

A. L. Rogers has been watching *Star Trek* for as long as he can remember. He is also an award-winning writer who has published short fiction in *Splickety* magazine, *Catapult* magazine, on DailyScienceFiction.com and elsewhere. Learn more about his books and other writing at andyrogersbooks.com and facebook.com/andyrogersbooks.